Milly and Roxy's
Summer in the Mitten

Dear Maya,

   Roxy and I would like to dedicate this story to you. We are sorry that you never got a chance to appear in one of our books. You were sweet and faithful to me and to our family. Thanks for teaching me the importance of barking at strangers and delivery trucks.

Love,
Marabou Milly

Maya

January 2001 – July 2014

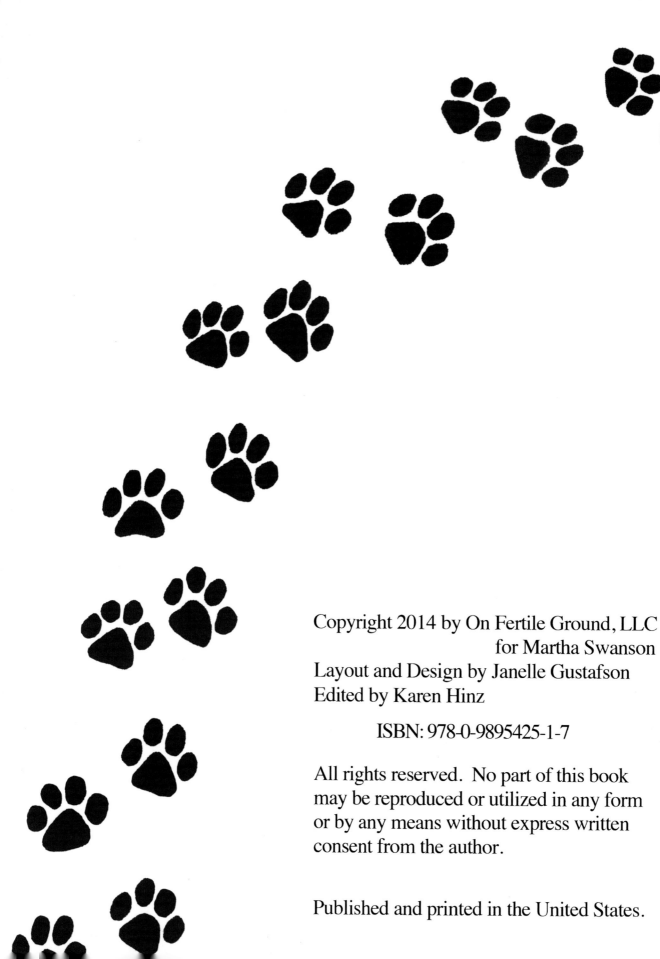

Copyright 2014 by On Fertile Ground, LLC
for Martha Swanson
Layout and Design by Janelle Gustafson
Edited by Karen Hinz

ISBN: 978-0-9895425-1-7

Published and printed in the United States.

Milly and Roxy's
Summer in the Mitten

Written by Martha Swanson
Illustrated by Meagan Lipke

I'm Milly, she's Roxy, she is my best friend.

We have Michigan adventures time and time again.

We went to school for the very last day.
Now it is summer! Hip Hip Hooray!

Our kids sleep in, so we go with the flow,
because all too soon, it's Up North they go.

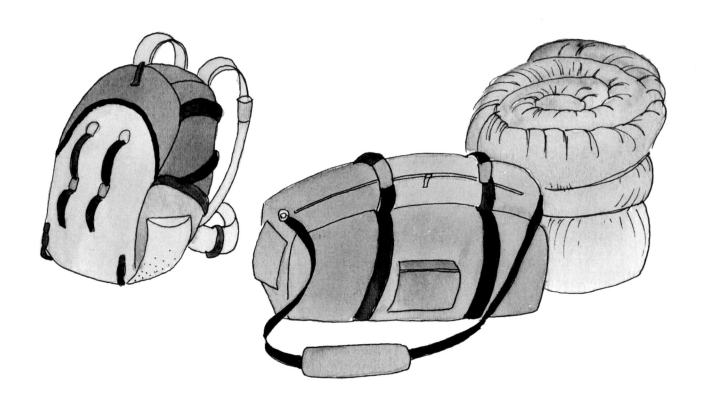

They're off to camp, and we go our own way,
where we're free to roam, to chase and to play.
While we're at the campfire, I sing along
with Roxy who's crooning a lovely new song.
I think we sound great when we sing a duet,
but no one asks us...I guess they forget.

We went all the way
to the Mackinac Bridge,
then down the coast
to a huge sandy ridge.

We romped and we raced as we made our way up
to the top where we found a tan scruffy pup.

She was all alone, and just a bit scared.
But Roxy and I, we're always prepared
to encourage new friends to share
in our fun. So Dixie joined in;
and that girl can RUN!

Back at the camp we tuck in for the night.
To lay beneath stars is a beautiful sight.

At 5 a.m. freighter horns start to blare.
"No peaceful slumber!" is what I declare.

The big lake can be stormy, or be very still
but I like it best when it gives me a thrill.
I choose to ride the waves in on a board.
Roxy does not, so she watches the shore.

I'm generally known as the strong and brave one.
When I hear fireworks, I turn and run.
I jump in a box, or cover my head.
Roxy consoles from the top of the bed.

In The Thumb we find a lively parade.
Peaches!
Bands!
Free Lemonade!
We go to festivals in towns large and small.
Most welcome dogs, and we have a ball.

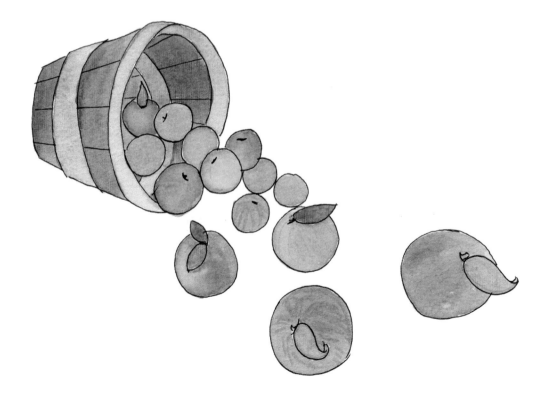

Next stop Detroit, to cheer on our team.
We're at the stadium, living our dream.
It is super fun to sit in the stands.
No hotdogs, just peanuts.
We're exceptional fans!

At the end of the summer, we're back in our town.
We've travelled the Mitten up hill and down.
It's time to get back to our school-year routines of
soccer and football. We've missed our home teams!

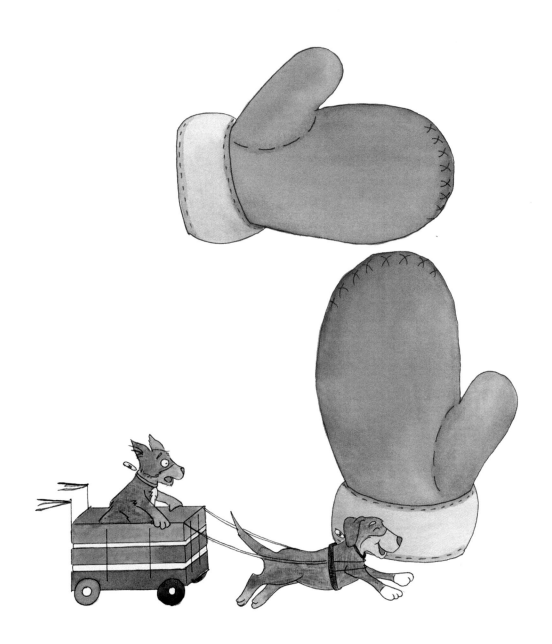

Look, Roxy, we've been all around this great state,

but this country's enormous: I just cannot wait
to see more mighty cities and small towns galore.
Lakes!
        Mountains!
                Rivers!
                        So much more to explore...

Some words about the main characters:

Martha Swanson

Martha and her husband, Don, love raising their three children in Clarkston, Michigan. Milly and Roxy have found their way into Martha's full life. Most of her working hours are dedicated to planting begonias and beautifying commercial properties, but the fact is, her favorite "work" is writing. Martha strives to prioritize faith and service to God and others. In the margin hours of her life, you might run into her riding her bike on a back road of Oakland County, Michigan or Chautauqua County, New York. Her other favorite ritual is sharing coffee with Don on the patio in the morning...just not too early.

Meagan Lipke

Meagan lives in Clarkston, Michigan with her extraordinary husband and three fun-loving kids. You'll often find her at a bonfire, teaching art in her classroom, pulling weeds in the garden, or throwing a frisbee at the dog park. Or, maybe you won't find her at all. She's prone to packing up the family and disappearing into the woods to wherever the trail leads. She also shares her home with her two dogs, Huckleberry and Magnolia, a little cat, four ducks, three floppy rabbits and an enormous number of chickens (who live outside, of course). This is her second book.

Marabou "Milly" chose the Swanson family on a fall day in 2011. She considers Chloe to be her master and trainer. She is a smart and capable, though often naughty, Terrier- Australian Shepherd mix. Her favorite day is spent in her backyard learning a new trick or playing tag with Roxy who really is her best friend.

Milly

Dixie

Real-life Dixie is a mixed breed pup, also from Clarkston, Michigan. She makes her home with the Wilson family and is appearing with Milly and Roxy in this, their summer book. It has been rumored that Dixie got stuck in a dune one time and had to be rescued by her owners.

Roxy

Roxy chose the Trim family in the Summer of 2012. She is loved and trained by Tracey. Roxy is a bit shy, but a well-behaved Miniature Australian Shepherd. Her favorite day is spent meeting up with Milly for a walk, or laying in the sun watching all the wildlife at Trim Pines.